Praise for *Letting Go Of*

First books are always exciting because it takes years, sometimes decades, for a writer to feel they've finally written enough well enough to have a book, and so by the time they convince themselves and someone else they have done just that, they have. In this book, Maeve Fox certainly has, providing luscious details of a life lived and felt deeply: grits and butter, crazy-ass birds, man cards, houses larger on the inside, kudzu, flowered dresses, and all one might need to feel and understand the love, loss, appreciation, growth, continuity, change and acceptance conveyed by these poems.

—Scott Owens, author of *eventually: haiku* and *An Augury of Birds*

Maeve Fox takes the trans experience into the Appalachians, wraps the pride flag around a hot bowl of grits (with butter!), and practices a hard earned self-acceptance and self-love that rural LGBTQ+ people need now more than ever. She has set her table with all the mismatched dishes and mason jars and memories, and invited us all to join her there, sit, and share a meal of poetry. Accepting her invitation will leave the reader all the richer for having done so.

—Jay Orlando, author of *A Tangled Lineage*

Letting
Go
Of
Me

A Collection of Poetry

John Fox
and
Maeve Fox

Letting Go of Me

Copyright © 2025 John Fox and Maeve Fox

All rights reserved. No part of this publication may be reproduced, distributed, or transmitted in any form or by any means, including photocopying, recording, or other electronic or mechanical methods, without the prior written permission of the publisher, except in the case of brief quotations embodied in critical reviews and certain other noncommercial uses permitted by copyright law. For permission requests, write to the publisher, addressed "Attention: Permissions Coordinator," at the address below.

ISBN: 978-1-959346-86-9 (Paperback)

Library of Congress Control Number: 2025933096

Cover Design (Art): Maeve Fox
Book Interior Design: Robert T Canipe

Printed in the United States of America.

First printing 2025.

Redhawk Publications
The Catawba Valley Community College Press
2550 Hwy 70 SE
Hickory NC 28602
https://redhawkpublications.com

To be nobody-but-yourself — in a world which is doing its best, night and day, to make you everybody else — means to fight the hardest battle which any human being can fight; and never stop fighting.

— e e cummings, "A Poet's Advice to Students"

Learning to let go should be learned before learning to get. Life should be touched, not strangled. You've got to relax, let it happen at times, and at others move forward with it.

— Ray Bradbury, "Farewell Summer"

This book is dedicated to my kids: Nathaniel, Sarah, Dylan and Khloe. You guys push me ever forward to be better. To my family that never knows how to quit. To my friends and lovers that have taught me that love has no limits. And to everyone who stood by me then and now. No matter how small the gesture, I see you.

To all the trans persons living in defiance of societal norms and fighting just to be yourselves. I see you and I love you.

Most especially, this book is dedicated to my husband, Jasper. I hope you are proud of this. I miss you so much it hurts.

Contents

Introduction	11
Assembling a Woman Over the Years	13
Grits and Butter	15
House of Hearts	16
Man Card	19
Brother	21
Crazy Ass Birds	23
Functional	24
Mountain Tales	26
I received a card	27
That song came on the radio	28
Caged	30
Theory	31
The Bird	32
Mountain Magic	33
Shopping for Flowered Dresses	34
Southern Girls Are Made of	36
No One	38
Repetition	39
Writer's Block	40
Something	41
Generally	42
Wildfires	43
Maestro	44
Of All the Things Before, After	45
Ode to Men I've Kissed	47
My Name	50
Euphoria	51
Deconstruction	52
Letting Go of Me	54
Acknowledgments	56
About the Author	57

Introduction

Over the years I have written a lot of poetry. I didn't realize how much until I started compiling this volume and the sheer weight of it was staggering. Not all of those poems are publish-worthy, for sure, but they do exist and they help tell a story that leads up to where I am at this point in my life.

Somewhere along the way, a major change happened. Many major changes happened, but this one was fundamental. I accepted who I was as a transgender woman.

This came with its own trials and tribulations, but it really struck me when I considered publishing the poetry I had written in the past. I had published one or two along the way, but now I wanted to put out a full book. What would I do with all these poems that felt like they were crafted by a different person?

It didn't feel right to change anything about them. Those poems were snapshots of a life that I valued dearly. It was, after all, still me, wasn't it?

I didn't have answers for a while and so I sat on it and honestly, I didn't write many poems in the beginning of that time. I was learning who this new me was. So many things were happening and there were so many experiences. New joy and new fears were everywhere.

I sat on it for a while as I am wont to do. I tend to move with deliberate steps, not making a move until I'm sure. I waited and thought and thought like Pooh Bear on a log in the Hundred Acre Wood.

Then, in 2021, my husband died in a car accident and the words of grief, loss and finally acceptance started to pour out of me. I began to realize that part of what held me back with my old work was the same feelings for the person I once was.

I decided that I would publish old work too and I would publish it under that old name one last time. This volume is a mix of his words and mine.

It's the story of learning to love, learning to lose and learning to change. It's my story.

This is about how I honor his words while I learn to let go and move forward.

Assembling a Woman Over Years

Some when,
a young boy holds hands
with a raven-haired boy.
He is enraptured by
a velvet skirt, silver jewelry,
by the freedom of make-up.
Weeks later, he finds his raven-haired boy
in a hallway with lips on a raven-haired girl.
His innocent heart breaks.

Some when,
A man holds a shaver, hands trembling.
Looking into blue eyes.
Excited and equally fearful.
The shaver buzzes across jawline,
Curled hair falls to the floor.
A woman looks up to meet her eyes
for the first time.

Some when,
A boy slides into the laundry closet.
He is alone in the house.
That makes him brave but,
he is *cautious*.
Purloining an item of clothing
he scurries to his room.
Takes a second to breathe.
He clumsily fastens a bra
around a flat, skinny chest.

Letting Go of Me

Some when,
A woman waits
in her mother's kitchen.
Today she isn't wearing makeup or wig.
She peels potatoes, building courage.
This day has been coming for months.
She knows that her mother loves her
no matter what.
It doesn't quell her fears.
Curled peels fall into the bag.
She says, *Mom I'm a woman*

Some when
A boy hears them call down the hall.
Hey faggot!
His blood runs cold. How?
How do they know that his lips
remember the taste
of that other boy's skin?
He pulls back long hair, readies his fists
waits for the beating.

Some when,
A woman steps out for the first time
fully realized.
Make-up done with novice skill.
Wig brushed, still uncomfortable.
Dress swishing around newly shaven legs.
Nerves jangling and dancing.
Her husband and daughter rush to hug her.
Everything falls into place.

Grits and Butter

Grits and butter are the taste of my memories.
Somewhere between porridge and rice
in consistency.
Not the dish for everyone, in fact,
some people hate them.
Grits and butter are just fine for me.

On lazy Sunday mornings there was always a
smell of breakfast cooking, and my mother
so happy to overload plates with
eggs, bacon, livermush, grits and biscuits.
One of the few times she was busy and content.
Cereal was reserved for school days.
Quick and sugary meals
we could make for ourselves
before rushing out to the bus.

It was Sunday where breakfast
became the heartbeat
of a family that was always on the go.
Grits and butter set the pace for the day.
Watching TV, playing outside,
or reading in the sun
started on days when that smell
wafted through the house.
More effective than revelry for getting
a horde of teenagers out of bed.
Even now grits and butter bring me back to
lazy Sundays when the world slowed down
and I pretended that it would always
be the five of us.

House of Hearts

The house I grew up in was larger on the inside.
It was a physics anomaly that
a three-bedroom house
(one bathroom)
once kept twelve people sheltered.
The wear and tear we put that house through,
I'm in constant awe that it still stands.

Every morning mom would wake us
in stages. Me first and then my brother.
Remind us to be quick, as the hot water heater
did not defy physics like the rest of the house.
It only held enough water for three showers
the late riser playing cold water roulette.

Our cabinets were filled to the brim with
mismatched plates.
Stacked in a precarious, leaning tower.
One Jenga pull away from a certain disaster.
Cereal was bought in bulk bags with knock off
characters. King Vitamin replaced the captain.
Some nameless lion replaced Tony the Tiger.
The fridge in the laundry room was kept
almost exclusively for gallons of milk.
Huddled around an old library table,
scratched and scarred
from use before we even got it,
we ate with a speed that no one could
imagine had they seen us just
twenty minutes earlier,
struggling to get out of bed.
Mom left for work before we all got on the bus
and got home well after school was over.

Letting Go of Me

In the afternoons the house was the domain of
homework and Ninja Turtles.
Twin girls fought over the remote as my brother
attempted to dribble a basketball
on a gravel drive.
As oldest, I attempted to wrangle them,
but my authority was always questioned
and mocked.

We waited, hungry hounds,
as dinner time crept near
and my exhausted mother came
through the door.
I'm sure there were days she dreaded the
maelstrom that she was about to enter.
Screaming mouths ready to eat,
my sister bursting to tattle about how one of us
hit or yelled at the other.

As a parent now, I know the deep breath
mom must have taken to help steel herself
right outside the front door,
already able to see the silhouettes
of tattletales and starving kids
that had at least one snack that afternoon,
if not two.

In the late night,
my mother would lay in the couch
grateful for a moment's silence
as all the children slept.
Even that silence was full
of soft sighs and snores.
The reprieve was bittersweet

Letting Go of Me

knowing that in a few
fleeting hours she would be forced
to do it all again.

I listen to the sounds of my own children,
creating the symphony of sleep.
I think back to that gentle,
harried woman and the strength
that she showed
by keeping that house together
firmly on her shoulders.
I'm awed and grateful
that she gave to us
the best years of her life.
She molded that pack of wild,
savage children into adults
on a budget of almost nothing
and a heart
that was bigger on the inside.

Man Card

They are going to take away my man card.
Another man held me in his arms and I
reveled in the feeling of not having to be strong,
for just a few minutes.
I breathed in deep the scent of him,
felt protected and secure.
So yeah, I'm gonna lose my man card.

I'm not sure when I got the card.
It could have been given to me when my dad
told me, M*en don't cry.*
When the leather of his belt hit my backside,
I was advised that it would be a lot worse
if I cried.

Maybe I got it when he said,
Art is fine but real men play sports.
If they knew that I loved the feeling of
a man's hard muscles against my skin,
my man card would be revoked.
It would have a big red stamp:
GAY
Because real men don't differentiate between
gay and bi-sexual.
If you like dick, you're a girl or you're gay.

I wish I could hand the damn card back in.
I wish I could rip it to shreds and cry.
Still tears won't come.
I've been an adult for longer than I was a child
and yet I've only cried four times
since I graduated high school.
I stood on the pulpit and tore my heart out

to read an elegy for my grandmother.
My eyes were dry.
Because men don't cry.
My teenage son hugs me and I feel awkward
instead of embracing him properly.
Because men don't goddamn cry.
Bipolar disorder drags me to the point of
wondering if my kids would be better off if I just
drove into oncoming traffic and I still don't cry.
Because men aren't pussies,
they suck it up and act tough.

The brand that was burned into me by this card
is so hard to put down
with all its rules and regulations.
Men stand up straight. Men provide.
Men don't let women and children see
vulnerability.
Men lock emotions up tight.
They must be the rocks of the family.
They are surprised when things finally reach
their breaking point.
Everything boils out in seething red hot anger.

Let's be real,
anger is a perfect emotion
if you are holding the man card.
Anger is strong, anger is powerful,
like an open hand across the face of a child
who *is too smart for his own damn good.*
Anger is seething disgust when the word
homosexual is brought up in conversation.
It's a gritted jaw and trail of spit that
flashes in the sun on its way to ground
before the words are spoken
Gays aren't natural.

Letting Go of Me

Brother

He calls himself Brother
this man at center stage inside a storm of hate.
He rails against gays and fornication and drugs,
screams about blasphemy and hell.
He stands ramrod straight, fists clenched,
as he spews his bile and anger onto the crowd.
This false prophet throws stones at the gathered
each with the name of God carved into them.
He does this in the name of Brotherhood.

My brother is a gentle man,
kind and quiet, quick to laugh, even at himself.
My brother has a presence so at peace
even animals can't sense his approach.
My brother is country sunsets and
early dew-covered mornings.
His is a message of life learned by living.

In sharp contrast is this Brother in front of me
His message comes from a book that he slaps.
Violently.
Every word is a weapon,
precise, sharp swords
meant to skewer victims,
spew blood upon the crowd.
His anger infects me.

Among his followers,
I am a wolf among the sheep.
Fists tight, face careful to mask my outrage.
How dare this man appropriate the title
Brother.
He cannot compare to the good man

Letting Go of Me

that shares my blood.
My teeth are machines grinding themselves to
nothing.
Venom backs up in my throat,
begging to be spewed forth.
My hate races to match his hate

Then I think of my brother and I am ashamed.
I step away from the crowd,
turn my back on the terrible words.
Let them fall off my back.
Clods of dirt tumbling to the ground in my wake.
Ahead of me there is a fishing trip,
long nights by a bonfire.

Crazy-Ass Birds

We stood in the backyard examining
the body of a tiny brown bird
that had shattered its fragile neck,
slamming into the solarium window.
What we have here is a crazy-ass bird,
my Paw-paw explained to me.
I was much too gullible
to see the sparkle of mischief
in his ancient eyes. That man
was my world.
I followed him around, thirsty for
every drop of knowledge he gave.

I picked up the bird and buried it,
before the cat made it into a meal.
Later on, I frantically scrambled
through the National Geographic book
of Wild Animals.
There was no mention of crazy-ass birds.
My Mee-maw wasn't nearly as amused
as he was when I told her what I was looking for.

I still imagine the crazy-ass bird,
flying into windows,
chasing reflections of itself.
Racing with all speed and no self-preservation.
Wings beating to match a frantic heart.
Resulting in nothing more than a thump
on a plate glass window.

Functional

I was asked to explain being functionally bipolar.
If I could function, they asked,
keep a job, be a husband and father.
Why couldn't other people?
As if a hierarchy existed for those
who could handle the world
and those who struggled.
I probably left some bullshit reply,
I don't remember, but it ate at me.

Functional- meaning able to do
things everyone else does.
Like waking up at 2 AM with crippling fear
of going into a job that I love.
Listening to the sounds of my wife
breathing while blood pounds in my ears.
My brain screaming, *I don't deserve this job.*
This life.

Being a functional bipolar I take showers
like everyone else, when I feel like it.
Drive to work and count how many times
my fingers itch to turn the wheel
into oncoming traffic.
47.
That's the highest number I've gotten to
when I kept track of the moments
I've considered suicide in one day.

Letting Go of Me

Functional bipolar is the moment you need
to call out of work because you just can't stand
to deal with people today,
but you have used all of your sick days already
and can't afford to not be there.
It's the feeling of terror you get when you know
there's work to be done, but you just can't
seem to focus on tomorrow,
or even ten minutes from now.
You need to get even one thing finished.
But you can't.

It is constantly being behind on work,
appointments, responsibilities.
The sheer anxiety of being an adult,
akin to being the tiny human swimming
frantically at the bottom of the tidal wave.
Yet when you look, other people surf
the wave with no problems.

Being functional bipolar is ignoring
the feeling that everyone you've ever met
hates you, because not doing so leads
you down deep paths of despair.
There is no escape.
Closing your eyes to ignore
as the voice of your father
whispers in your ear,
What a disappointment you are
even though you haven't talked to him
in months.

Mountain Tales

The wind howls around the cabin,
Wrapping around the shutters,
a spectral hand rattling the windows.
I lay in bed with my grandfather.
Eight years old and listening
to an invisible monster try and get in
as my Pawpaw peacefully snores.

My mind racing with stories
of haints and wampuses.
Creatures conjured from tall tales
he had told me in whispered tones.
I hung on every word in reverent awe
anxious to believe in magic and monsters.
In the night, the terrible creature
tries to get in and gobble me up
while I huddle as close as I can
to his warm, steady body.
Knowing he will protect me from demons
he had conjured earlier in the evening.

In the morning, snow covers the cabin.
Bright, pure and soft.
I look for tracks,
evidence of any night haunt,
and of course, find none.
Nevertheless, I still listen close,
when the wind blows
and monsters prowl the mountain tops.

I received a card.

The passing of a year
I waited on your call
I received a card
I asked for your love
I pined for acceptance
I received a card
I inspect myself inside out
trying to find the reason you don't want me
I received a card
I beg and plead for any sign of pride
Spent that night lying awake
wondering what I did wrong
I received a card
I watch my children not know you
I swallow the lump of bitter anger
I received a card
I hope that maybe you feel guilt
Your gut all twisted
when you think of us
I received a card
I didn't want anything more than a talk
Just dinner and a laugh, *hi how are you*
I received a card
I accept that you have a another life
I hope they don't disappoint you
I received a card
I know you'll never read this
The status quo remains
Maybe next year
I'll receive another card

The song came on the radio

The one that goes...
                        Well, you know how it goes.
It brought me back to a soft summer night
In the back of the car, seats laid down.
Naked legs wrapped in Gordian knots.
I fell in love with you in the moonlight.
As you touched my face and said,
                    Everything is going to be ok.

The song came on the radio
The one that goes....
                        Well, you know how it goes.
When we danced in the kitchen
Of our very first home.
I struggled to find the rhythm.
You took the lead.
I fell in love with you again,
on that gray linoleum floor
Your hand touched my hip. You said,
        Just do what I do. It'll make sense.

The song came on the radio
The one that goes...
                        Well, you know how it goes.
We were flying down the deserted highway
at 5AM. The sun struggling to meet the night.
My fingers bone white on the wheel.
You wrapped your strong and steady hands
around mine, turned the radio up,
rolled down the window and sang.

The song came on the radio.
The one that goes...

Letting Go of Me

                Well, you know how it goes.
I looked over to find you.
There was only an urn on the dresser
the most precious green and gold.
It reminded me of the song.
The one for you and me.
The one that goes...
                Well, you know how it goes.

Caged

Keep the tiger in a cage.
See it pace the floor.
Watch golden eyes calculate distance.
Muscled killer wrapped in velvet trim.

Keep the tiger in a cage.
Know it is without fear.
Hear its steady breath.
Vicious fangs behind soft, wet lips.

Keep the tiger in a cage
Until one day it is free.
Feel its teeth.
Feel its claws.
Feel muscles,
descend upon you.

Theory

The words make sense
before they leave my mouth.
I'm not sure what happens in the space
between thought and speech.
I guess they get shuffled and twisted by time.
One second to next, things change on a dime.
Are we the same as we were back then?
You know what I mean,
before these words began.
Or is each second a universe in itself,
and there are sixty of me and sixty of you,
every minute
And if we live in a quantum flux, a juxtaposition
of minutes and dimensions,
Should we hold onto what was said
just a second ago?
Probably not, but we do it for show.
Sixty me and sixty of you, every minute, means
sixty thoughts, and sixty emotions,
all of that leaves,
sixty words left unspoken.
Everything makes sense before it
stumbles off my tongue,
and falls into sixty reasons why it all comes out wrong.

The Bird

A bird was trapped in my house the other day.
Its wings beat frantic patterns as it
swooped and whirled
from corner to corner.
It perched high on the shelves,
letting out a cry that I recognized in a place
deep within.
It was the sound my heart made
when a friend asked,
How are you holding up?
and what I needed was to say,
Nothing is the same.
I am changed by force,
by the violence
Of a car slamming into another car
that I wasn't even inside.
My life from one second to the next
was rendered inert.
But what I say is, *As well as can be expected.*
Because no one truly wants
to be opened up to your pain.
They ask genuinely, but with no concept
of how twisting metal and shattered glass
echo in your soul.
As gently as I can,
I gathered the bird in a towel,
carried him outside
into freedom,
and released him.

Mountain Magic

When I say that I can sense a storm coming,
it is because I am a woman born and raised
in the Appalachian hills and valleys.
I can smell the rain in the air before
the first drops caress my skin.
The soil on the hill tops, grey and musty.
The clay of the foothills, red and heavy.

There are scientific words like petrichor,
to me it will always be mountain magic.
I can feel the pressure of the coming storm.
Baring down in heavy waves along
my freckled shoulders and arms.

It's a sixth sense honed by years
of getting caught in sudden summer showers
while I danced in the woods,
my face turned toward the Heavens
like the leaves around me,
supplicants asking the sky
for the cool cleansing gift
sent from the clouds on a summer day.

Often the mountains hide the horizon from view,
especially in deep valley shade.
Summer storms come up
fierce and fast upon the unsuspecting.
Those of us with magic in our veins and
mountain between our toes
have enchanted our senses into weathervanes
more accurate than the man
on the news channel.

Shopping for Flowered Dresses

I look longingly at the dresses in the store
As I pass
Again and Again.
I circle the store, pretending to look at various items
As I scan for how many
Women are also shopping.
I make a plan, noting which items
I want to look at as I drift by.

When the time comes, I am hawk-quick.
Striking my flowered prey so fast
No one has time for disapproving glances
or angry huffs.
My hands move with practiced speed.
Rifling through fabric to find my size.
I have to hope that they will fit.
Dressing rooms become panic rooms
if I am alone.
I will stay for too long, listening to make sure
I am not ambushed on the way out.

The space between the women's section
and checkout is a gauntlet.
Self-checkout is a safe haven from
the eye rolls and sucking teeth
of a cashier,
as I try not to make eye contact.
Some days I am strong enough to
stare them down.
Not today.

Letting Go of Me

My friends think I am a bastion of strength.
Deflecting micro aggressions like
Wonder Woman's enchanted bracelets.
Wearing audacity as armor is exhausting.

Southern Girls Are Made Of

I am constructed of thorns and briars.
The kind that rip jeans and leave reminders
in sharp stings across roving hands.
I am thick underbrush in the way,
hiding mysteries on the forest floor.
I am warning signs that the way forward
is wild and dangerous.

I am wrapped in creeping flowered vines.
Thick and sweet.
Lingering in the air, and haunting minds
long after I am gone.
I am flowers, thriving in the wild
and wilting quickly in confinement.
I am the scent of laughter on the wind,
the beam of sun that lulls you into a nap
on a warm afternoon.

I am barefoot on hot summer asphalt,
never standing still, dancing across obstacles.
I am thick calluses that shield away
heat and the burrs that I come across.
I am brave and fearless,
willing to take on any challenge.
I am my Momma's stubborn side.
Even when I know hurt is gonna come
I'll step out on that parking lot.

Letting Go of Me

I am a Southern girl.
We were never meant to be sugar and spice.
We are sharp grit and gravel.
We are soft flowers and lace.
We are fierce smiles and quick wit.
We are built between
mountains and sea.
We are what our Mommas and Mee-maws
shaped us to be.

No One

no one in my bed this morning
no one breathing on my pillow
no one smiling as sun slants down
no one laughing at whispered teasing
no one touching me oh so softly
no one kissing my lips this morning
no one pair of pants (not mine) on my floor
no one telling me they love me
no one
until you come back

Repetition

With the reality of a disconnected number
It comes to mind I am much too late.
As the automated voice advises hanging up
and trying again.
I do.
Repetition is insanity.

While holding on to the off chance
you might be there.
I drove by our favorite place time and again.
Someone else has taken that spot.
They can have it.
Just in case, I circle again.
Repetition is insanity.

Writer's Block

here i am precarious limb
words poised on the brink of birth
hide from me whatever their worth
lie to me with silvered-tongue
page beginning to swell and fill
hard for me to control the spill
tumbling babble inside my head
thundering release felt, not said
traitorous words won't let feelings hide
snickering syllables sneak past my eyes
emotions escape in alphabet disguise
the work almost done, there's little left now
defeated and beaten, i silently weep
for paragraphs and sentences i couldn't keep
here is my heart written in ink
betraying fingers leapt before I could think

Something

Something doesn't work anymore,
The cogs don't cog, the gyros don't gyrate.
Something isn't right.
The colors spin out of sync.
The words tumble down.
Something doesn't keep time anymore.
The music's off key, melody not soothing.
Something isn't in place anymore.
The Something, could be Nothing,
Something might all be a dream,
But I think the Something that isn't meshing.
The Something that isn't flowing,
That Something might be me.

Generally

There is no one knocking at the door.
It's not a surprise he's been there before.
There is someone dancing in my heart.
I'm not worried she knows her part.
Without anyone to show me the way,
I find that I'm learning more every day.
And old mr no one, who stands outside,
wants nothing more than to reside,
with anyone, so he won't be so alone.
While I'm waiting for someone
to just pick up the phone.

Wildfires

wildfires burn in the hills
dance in the trees
roar, devour, consume
stampeding beasts,
panicking birds
the sky alive
flames and wings
aftermath chills
skeleton sentinels
blackened, twisted,
smoldering, smoking
ash filled air
everything dead and still

Maestro

I know that taste.
How salty sweet it is.
Wraps round my tongue,
like oh so much honey.
Beautiful lie, that floats on a melody,
straight from my lips to your spiraling ear.
A perfection of craft,
a masterpiece of deception.
Spun like cotton candy, at the fair in September.
I'll feel it, when the stickiness traps me.
I know that taste.
How bitter it is.
After it's over,
and the sweetness has worn off.

Of All the Things Before, After and In Between

When I say that I love you,
what I mean is that I want to love you like kudzu
loves an old house in a field.
Which is to say that I want to wrap around you,
so tight,
that no one else can access you,
without going through me.
I want to consume you in my deep green life,
and hide you from every hurt.
You see, lots of things I've loved have moved on,
from me,
from the situation,
from this life.
My desire is to grow around you in such a way
that we are
        inseparable,
        indistinguishable.

When I say that I love you,
what I mean is that, I am a fish
struggling to swim past a large dam
that has been erected directly in my path.
When I was young, love tried to crush me
under the weight of another's love for themself.
I nearly drowned under the waters of her
presence, willing to surrender my last breaths
to prove myself.
And so, when I say that I love you,
what I mean is that,
I am
        dying.

Letting Go of Me

When I say that I love you,
What I mean is that I will love you
 like planets in orbit.
A space where inconsistency is the struggle
between the gravity of affection and the comfort
of the cold independence of stars
blinking in the void.
I will cherish you at the apogee of my orbit,
and pine for the cold when I am in your arms.
Which is not to say that I do not want you,
more that love has always
been fraught with meteors,
which leave craters in my soul, until
I no longer resemble myself.

When I say that I love you,
what I mean is that I am terrified.
Terrified of love,
    Of you,
    Of Me,
    Of all the things
        before,
                      after
          and
          in between.

Ode to men I have kissed

I.

You were sweet in your own way,
more experienced than I,
though a year younger.
My hands fumbled at your buttons.
I remember tracing my lips across
your jawline,
Adam's apple
Collar bone.
Too enamored to feel the fear
that would come later
as I realized the implications of
being queer in a small rural town.
Afterwards I pretended that we had never
touched. You were the first person
I truly hurt.

II.

To describe you in a way that brings justice
is impossible.
We were both sharing a prison
we could not escape.
Love coming from a sense of desperation.
A need to have any control when the
puppet strings started to
tug and we had to dance.
Her honeyed words dripping onto us, as our lips
begged each other to find escape.
Years later we would kiss for the last time,
silent and passionate.

Letting Go of Me

III.

We were in your bed,
bodies entwined like vines.
Your leg was on top of mine,
holding me down,
with my face close to yours,
You tossed words like piercing needles
gently spoken but deadly nonetheless.
Why can't you admit that you are a queer?
Bisexuals just need to get off the fence.
Afterwards you got up,
and I cried, as you pissed with the door open.

IV.

Fast forward a good bit,
to man so gentle and nervous.
Roles reversed from that first boy,
and the tender, guiding kiss
I had shamefully rejected years ago.
I was still new to womanhood
You were exploring queerness.
Your kisses were questioning and worried.
I could feel your shiver as you fumbled around
how to love a trans body.
Orpheus terrified that if he said the wrong thing
his Euridice would vanish into the darkness.

V.
Two people still discovering who
they were, and what roles they should occupy
in the queerest of quandaries.
Passion that was both
confident and gentle,
leaving space for uncertainty.
Our bodies in mid metamorphosis,
stuck in an awkward stage
that felt like teenagers, even though
we were clearly
adults.

Afterwards I cried in your arms.

My Name

My name is an ancient ritual
Bound to ancestor blood and bone.
My name is a tether to the past,
A reminder of where I came from.
My name invokes a man
who was my whole world.
My name is changing.
It is part of a metamorphosis I can't resist.
If I'm no longer who I was,
Who am I?
My new name fits this form like water.
My new name shifts and shimmers
northern lights calling me onward.
My old name is not a discarded cicada shell,
left to wither in the summer heat.
My new name did not swallow the old.
It grew up around it like thick honeysuckle.
Sweet and powerful.

Euphoria

The swish of a skirt around legs,
freshly shaven.
Remembering what it feels like to have hair
brush my shoulders.
The jingle of earrings dangling and dancing
with my walk
The sound of someone saying my name
with love in their heart.
The smell of dark purple lipstick,
Applied carefully.
The way my scent has changed over time.
The slight swell of breasts and hips blooming.
The feeling of a brain buzzing correctly.
All the proper chemicals flowing through.
Letters from lovers, with my name printed
in a flowing script.
Flowers in a vase, and not being afraid to admit
that I love pretty things.
Seeing how proud my daughter is of me,
as I learn to allow myself to be the person
I always should have been.

Deconstruction

Standing in front of the mirror
at the end of the day.
Slowly I wipe away my makeup,
I think about the man who called me sir,
despite my flowered dress.
Every swipe of the cloth reveals
stubble, wide jaw, thick chin.
    One,
        Two
            Three
                Four
My earrings hit the counter like gunshots.
I can see my old name on every bill
that comes to the house.
      Mr. in bold text.
I carefully take off my wig,
brush it out and put it on the stand.
You don't seem like one of those trannys
says the guy in my dating app.
I lift my dress up over my head, exposing
    round tummy
      small breasts.
Still some hair left that I'll have to shave later.
My aunt says, *Are you going to date men now?*
I don't know how to answer.
I pull off my bra, stretch in small relief.
My boobs aren't big enough to really need one,
but the nipples make a scene if I don't.
I stare for a while at my naked self in the mirror,
    no makeup
        clothes
            wig
                jewelry.

Letting Go of Me

Sometimes she's so hard to see,
through the receding hairline,
and wide shoulders.
But then I notice that quick sparkle in my eyes.
The touch of a smile on my lips.

And everything else fades into the background.

Letting Go of Me
(*a letter to John*)

When I moved back to my hometown
I hoped no one would know me.
Of course, they did.

I want so desperately to shed this skin
and emerge with butterfly perfection.
Changing your name, the way you dress
doesn't erase insecurities
carried through years.
You occupied this space for so long.
I'm a new tenant,
rummaging around in the attic
with half-forgotten remnants
of a life that
resembles someone else's home movies.

Every time someone shouts,
Didn't we go to school together?
My blood runs cold. I steel myself for
the inevitable barrage of questions.
Each one leading to the dreaded,
What is this all about?
With a gesture that encompasses…
everything.
I chat about your life, your memories,
your victories, your mistakes.

Letting Go of Me

All I want is to create something of my own,
but the luggage still has your name on it.
The further I move from you,
it feels like a weird dream I had.
One of those where you wake up groggy,
and it's hard to tell which reality you are in.

I can't hide or forget every little reminder
of a life you lived and I spectated.
I will let you go, write you into the past,
a ghost name on a book that sits on the shelf.
When I need to, I can pull it out,
read those words,
and remember,
when I used to be a boy.

Acknowledgments

I'd like to thank Scott Owens, and Leslie Rupracht for helping mentor me through the process of creating this book and providing space for everyone to read regardless of orientation.

To Redhawk Publications and Patty Thompson for giving my words a chance to be heard.

To my writing group and Jay Orlando for helping me refine my work and become a better writer.

To my family both by blood and by choice for believing in me the whole way. It has taken a long time to get here and I would never have done it without you.

About the Author

Maeve Fox is a native of Western North Carolina and has been writing poetry for over 20 years. She, like many people did, transitioned in 2020 during the COVID pandemic, and has been adjusting to her new life ever since. She is a mediator at a non-profit. She also loves Tabletop RPGS, and is a regular on several actual play streams and podcasts. If asked, she will give you a 4-hour lecture on the X-men.

Made in the USA
Columbia, SC
30 March 2025